Groundhog's Dilemma

Groundhog's Dilemma

Kristen Remenar

Illustrated by Matt Faulkner

Charlesbridge

For our kids: Julia, Joe, Chelsea, and Gabriel
—K. R. & M. F.

For Matt, always
—K. R.

Published by Charlesbridge
85 Main Street
Watertown, MA 02472
(617) 926-0329
www.charlesbridge.com

Library of Congress Cataloging-in-Publication Data
Remenar, Kristen, author.
  Groundhog's dilemma/Kristen Remenar ; illustrated by Matt Faulkner.
    pages cm
  Summary: Groundhog wants to please all the animals, but half of them want spring
to come quickly and the other half do not—and all of them think he controls the seasons,
so what is a poor groundhog to do on Groundhog Day?
  ISBN 978-1-58089-600-9 (reinforced for library use)
  ISBN 978-1-60734-903-7 (ebook)
  ISBN 978-1-60734-904-4 (ebook pdf)
1. Woodchuck—Juvenile fiction. 2. Animals—Juvenile fiction. 3. Groundhog Day—Juvenile
fiction. 4. Spring—Juvenile fiction. 5. Ethical problems—Juvenile fiction. 6. Friendship—
Juvenile fiction. [1. Woodchuck—Fiction. 2. Forest animals—Fiction. 3. Groundhog Day—
Fiction. 4. Spring—Fiction. 5. Seasons—Fiction. 6. Conduct of life—Fiction.
7. Friendship—Fiction.] I. Faulkner, Matt, illustrator. II. Title.
PZ7.R2828Gr 2015
813.6—dc23   2014010493

Printed in China
(hc) 10 9 8 7 6 5 4 3 2 1

Illustrations done in pencil, watercolor, and gouache on Arches 140-lb. cold-press watercolor paper
Display type set in Blue Century by Chicago www.t26.com
Text type set in Hunniwell by GHH & WR at Aah Yes Fonts and Family Dog by Jakob Fischer
Color separations by Colourscan Print Co Pte Ltd, Singapore
Printed by 1010 Printing International Limited in Huizhou, Guangdong, China
Production supervision by Brian G. Walker
Designed by Diane M. Earley

"I see my shadow!" Groundhog declared.
Half the animals cheered. The other half groaned.

Groundhog's shoulders slumped. "I just call it like I see it," he mumbled, heading back into his den for a good, long nap.

Spring finally arrived, and everyone came out to look for food.

The next morning Squirrel stopped by for a visit.
"Groundhog, my pal! Want to sit with me at the
ball game today? I'll share my peanuts," he said.
"Really? Gee, thanks!" replied Groundhog.

“Anything for a friend! Maybe next February you could return the favor by making spring come early,” Squirrel suggested.

That afternoon Bear clapped a paw on Groundhog's shoulder.

"How would you like to play catch after the game?" Bear offered.

"I don't know. . . . Usually you get mad because I keep dropping the ball," Groundhog said.

WIGGLEY FIELD

TICKETS

"Well, today I'm in a good mood. And if I get six extra weeks of sleep next winter, I'll be in a good enough mood to teach you how to throw!" Bear replied.

Really, all I do is—

Just before the game began, Sparrow called out encouragingly to Groundhog. "I'm sure we can find a position for the guy who can make spring come early."

Groundhog opened his mouth to protest, but he looked longingly at the team warming up.

Want to play?

Me?

As he settled in for the winter, Groundhog felt restless. One snowy night he left his den, looking for help.

"Owl," said Groundhog, "I need some advice. Squirrel and Sparrow want an early spring, but Hare and Bear want a longer winter. I've said yes to everyone because I want them to like me."

I don't control the weather—I just predict it.

"Ah, to see or not to see your shadow, that is the question," said Owl. "You got yourself into this, Groundhog. You'll have to get yourself out."

Groundhog slunk back to his den. He spent several restless weeks mulling over his options before sinking into an uneasy sleep.

February 2 dawned chilly and bleak. Groundhog looked up at the partly cloudy sky. He looked around at the expectant faces. He looked down at the ground, unsure of what he saw.

Do you see your shadow or not?

Groundhoggy . . .

Then the sun broke free of the clouds and shone brightly. Groundhog knew that no matter what he said, spring would come when it wanted to, and either way, someone would be angry. All he could do was tell the truth.

Six more weeks of winter!

So Groundhog took a deep breath and puffed up his chest. "I see my shadow!" he announced.
Half the animals cheered. The other half groaned.

GROUNDHOG

"We *are* friends! You're all my friends! So I . . ."
Groundhog sighed. "I promised you what you
wanted so you would stay friends with me."

Groundhog hung his head. "I'm sorry, everyone.
I shouldn't have pretended that I could control the
weather. I just call it like I see it. That's all."

It's not because of your job that we're your friends.

Well, not *only* because of it. . . .

Groundhog looked up at them, grumpy and hungry from months of cold. "I know it doesn't make what I did right, but maybe you'd like to join me for hot chocolate and snacks?" he asked.

Six weeks will go by faster with a full stomach.

With some grumbling and squeezing, everyone joined Groundhog. They ate, talked, and laughed until they were stuffed and sleepy again.

Back to the den . . .

PORRIDGE

"Sparrow?" Groundhog said. "I know you're angry, but I'd still like to play baseball with you in the spring."

Sparrow smiled. "We could use a good umpire."

Groundhog grinned. "I'll call it like I see it."

I am what I am.
Popeye